W9-CCI-778

Dog Watch

BOOK ONE

Trouble in Pembrook

Dog Watch

BOOK ONE

Trouble in Pembrook

By Mary Casanova

Illustrated by Omar Rayyan

Aladdin Paperbacks

New York   London   Toronto   Sydney

If you purchased this book without a cover, you should be aware
that this book is stolen property. It was reported as "unsold
and destroyed" to the publisher, and neither the author nor
the publisher has received any payment for this "stripped book."

This book is a work of fiction. Any references to historical events,
real people, or real locales are used fictitiously. Other names,
characters, places, and incidents are the product of
the author's imagination, and any resemblance
to actual events or locales or persons,
living or dead, is entirely coincidental.

ALADDIN PAPERBACKS
An imprint of Simon & Schuster
Children's Publishing Division
1230 Avenue of the Americas, New York, NY 10020
Text copyright © 2006 by Mary Casanova
Illustrations copyright © 2006 by Omar Rayyan
All rights reserved, including the right of reproduction
in whole or in part in any form.
ALADDIN PAPERBACKS and colophon are
trademarks of Simon & Schuster, Inc.
Designed by Tom Daly
The text of this book was set in Gazette.
Manufactured in the United States of America
First Aladdin Paperbacks edition April 2006
2 4 6 8 10 9 7 5 3 1
Library of Congress Control Number 2005924393
ISBN-13: 978-0-689-86810-8
ISBN-10: 0-689-86810-3

Dedicated to

the dogs of Ranier, Minnesota—
past, present, and future

And

to Kate, Eric, and Charlie—
and the dogs who have brought
tears and trouble, love and
laughter over the years

True:

On the edge of a vast northern Minnesota lake sits a quiet little village where dogs are allowed to roam free. Free, that is, until they get in trouble. One report of a tipped garbage can, nonstop barking, or car chasing, and the village clerk thumbs through *DOGGY MUG SHOTS*, identifies the dog from its photo, and places a colorful round sticker on the culprit's page. Then she phones the dog's owner. Too many stickers and the troublesome dog is ordered to stay home—tethered to a chain or locked in its yard. No more roaming, no more adventures with the other dogs of the village.

To the Fire Hydrant

Every morning, after Kito and Chester shared a heaping bowl of Hearty Hound, they sat by their owners—the Hollinghorsts—for a good round of scratching. Then they pawed at the back door and set off for adventure.

"They're good dogs," said Mrs. H.

"You bet," agreed Mr. H.

Kito paused and glanced back at the cedar-shingled house. From the doorway Mr. and Mrs. H watched them go. She was still in her dragonfly pajamas, and he carried his favorite coffee mug, the red one

1

with little white paw prints and the words "It's a Dog's Life." She was an artist, he was a writer. Stay-at-home owners. The best kind a dog could have.

Kito would give his life for the Hollinghorsts, though honestly, they had no clue what really went on with their dogs. People never heard dogs talk. People had to open their mouths to speak, but dogs could carry on a conversation without yapping their jaws. Barking, whining—those were ways of communicating—and silent speaking, another means entirely.

A hedge of purple lilacs scented the morning air. Hummingbirds zipped through coral bells. Kito dashed ahead to the dock, where Chester was sniffing the wood planks with his black nose. *Snuffle, snuffle, snuffle.*

"No dog has a better nose than you, Chester, but anytime we get a lead on something, your snuffling and snorting gives us away. No wonder we never catch any squirrels or chipmunks!"

"Jumpin' jitters, otters were here last night!" Chester said, weaving back and forth and snuffling along the dock. "Looks like they're gone now."

"I could have told you that," Kito said.

"That otters were here?"

"No, that they're gone now—by just using my eyes."

"Someday I'll show you what my nose can do," Chester said with an extra-loud snort.

3

"I'm not holding my breath, buddy."

With a piercing squawk, a seagull swooped low over Kito's head and he flattened himself to the dock, tail between his legs. "Wh-what was that?"

Chester laughed as the seagull flew over to the mayor's dock and perched on a wooden post. "Criminy biscuits, Kito! You'd probably be scared of a mouse's shadow."

Kito stood and shook his coat. "That's pretty low. I admit, I got a little nervous, but I thought it was an eagle—"

"Ha. As if an eagle could carry *you* away. You must weigh, what—eighty pounds?"

"Sixty-three at my last vet check." He turned away, his tail curved once again over his back instead of hanging low in fear. "Hey, enough already, Chester the Pester."

Dock checked, the dogs drank from the lake as a freight train rumbled and hummed across the lift bridge. Many trains passed over the bridge from Canada into their little Minnesota village.

Together the dogs scouted out the

boundaries of their yard and marked their territory.

"Y'know," Chester said, "though we scare otters, seagulls, chipmunks, and squirrels away—a duty that keeps us busy—sometimes I think we're not making full use of our skills. After all, beagles like me were bred for serious hunting and tracking, and, well, you might be a mutt, but Mr. and Mrs. H always say you're half chow chow, which gives you some sort of royal dog blood."

"Something like that. My ancestors guarded the emperors of ancient China and were bred for their intelligence and courage." Kito knew he had inherited extra smarts—it was courage he was short on.

"Okay, yard checked," said Kito, his stately amber tail arched high. "Let's head to the hydrant."

Every morning they headed to the fire hydrant outside the post office. The hydrant was the place to gather the latest news, at a time that village dogs could count on. After that it was vet checks, shopping trips, appointments with Mrs. Mertz, the dog groomer, and errands with owners. Things that got in the way.

The pavement was warm under Kito's paws. His thick coat was already too warm in the morning sun. As he trotted down Pine Street, he knew this day was going to be different. It wasn't just his scare at the dock. Something about the morning felt different. Kito couldn't put his paw on it exactly. Maybe it was the heat, but his instincts told him differently. Chester might have a keener sense of smell, but Kito had learned to trust his gut. A jittery nervousness fluttered in his belly.

Some kind of *trouble* was definitely in the air.

Trouble in Pembrook

The fresh coats of paint on the community building—blue trim on white—made Kito's nose twitch. Near the street, Mrs. Burkowski, the village clerk, stood at the base of a ladder; on the top rung teetered Mr. Cutler in his paint-splattered overalls. With his hammer he tacked up a corner of a large banner that spanned telephone pole to telephone pole over Main Street.

"Morning, Kito . . . Chester," Mr. Cutler called.

"Morning, fellows," added Mrs. Burkowski.

"Want a treat?" She scurried into the community building and returned with bone-shaped dog biscuits. "Here you go."

The dogs chewed their snacks, then waited to see if she'd bring more.

"I just put this banner up yesterday," said Mr. Cutler.

Mrs. Burkowski squeezed her empty hands into her jeans' back pockets. "Why the heck would someone rip it down? Maybe someone has something against our celebration."

"Must be tourists or teenagers," Mr. Cutler said. "Or someone with a grudge."

"Well, Mr. Cutler, keep a lookout for any more signs of troublemaking and I'll certainly do the same."

Kito studied the street banner: Pembrook Village Celebration, June 21st!!! He was the only village dog who could read, something he aimed to keep secret. He didn't want the other dogs to get their snouts bent out of shape. Smart was one thing. Show-offy was another. Most dogs understood people: their conversations, bits of radio and TV. But somewhere along the way, beyond listening, Kito had started to make sense of printed words, and sometime before the Hollinghorsts rescued him from the pound, he was already reading.

"Hey, Kito—c'mon," Chester said, standing square from his little black nose to his pointed tail. At his full beagle height, Chester stood no taller than Kito's shoulder. Sun glistened off Chester's long, silky ears as he tossed his head impatiently. "Good gravy, Kito! Everybody's waiting."

Kito shifted his gaze to the post office, where a half dozen dogs clustered around the fire hydrant, all sniffs and wags. "Sorry, I was lost in thought."

"Only two things worth thinking about," said Chester.

"And what might those two things be, Mr. AKC?" asked Kito.

Despite a severe overbite, Chester was always harping about his American Kennel Club certificate posted on the fridge and boasting that he was probably the only *true purebred* in the whole village.

"Sniffing," Chester said, "and food."

"And one more thing," Kito said. "Strangers."

"Criminy," Chester said. "Here we go again."

Kito drew a deep breath. "If this year's celebration is anything like the last, the village will soon be overcrowded with new people. And *strangers*—with all their new smells, sounds, ways of walking and behaving—put me on edge. I can't help it. My legs start quivering, then my back hairs stand up. And once that starts, I'm torn between my instincts—to attack and protect, or to get the heck out of there."

Chester stood nose to nose with him. "Listen, you already have two red stickers on your chart at the village clerk's office. So get a grip."

"I know, I know. I growled once at Mavis, the postmaster, but she was wearing a parka with a fur-trimmed hood that snowy day. She'd scared the bones out of me—hadn't recognized her at all! And at last year's festival I nipped the air when that woman tried to drag me by my collar to meet her kids. But I didn't actually bite her—just warned her. I mean, she was a complete *stranger.* What did she expect? I ran home to safety and stayed on the cool cement floor beneath Mr. H's workbench. My luck. She reported me, just the same."

"Just be careful," Chester said. "One more sticker and you could be forced to stay home—for good!"

"I know." Kito gave his coat a twitch, trying to wiggle off his worry, and followed Chester. As he did, his shadow trotted beside him like a fluffy fox.

Fire Hydrant News

The yellow fire hydrant on the corner held a zillion messages in code: who had been there, who was new, or who was in a bad mood. Six dogs clustered around it, talking all at once.

Running free carried its risks, which more than doubled when strangers drove through Pembrook. Every so often tragedy struck. Joining the other dogs was the village's most recent survivor: Lucky. A golden retriever with a white star on her chest—and now three legs instead of four—

she had been at home recovering after getting struck by a speeding car last month.

"Lucky!" Chester called, darting to her side. "You're back!"

"Hello, friend!" Kito added.

Though Lucky's right hind leg was gone, she still was able to sit on her haunches. "I'm glad to be back, believe me."

Chester butted his snout into the throng of dogs. "So, what's the skinny?"

"The what?" Schmitty cocked his black Lab ears.

"The low down," said Chester. "You know, what's going on? You were all talking at once so it must be important. Here—let me guess. Tundra's put one of you in your place again, teeth to your throat, am I right?"

"Nooope." Gunnar, the basset hound, smacked his drooping jowls. He talked the same way he walked. One speed, and it wasn't fast. "Haven't seeeeeen her yet." Skin sagged around his bloodshot eyes. A slippery strand of drool hung from the corner of his mouth, and when he shook his head and long ears, goop splattered the sidewalk.

Chester continued. "Okay, let me try again. You're all fighting about Willow, that new cute dog."

"If she goes for any dog, it will be me," Schmitty said, holding his tail extra high, his mouth wide and grinning. The runt of his littermates, Schmitty was friendly with everyone in the village.

Kito held back, watching and listening. Villagers stopped by on foot, on bikes, or in cars, heading in and out of the post office with bundles of mail tucked under their arms. They chatted with one another pretty much the same way the dogs did.

Muffin, a tiny fluffball sporting a purple bandanna, spoke up. "What's up," she said, "is that Tundra's gone missin'—and somethin' 'bout that is settin' our paws all a jiggin'."

"Muffin," Chester said, shaking his head, "where did you learn to speak?"

"Told you, I ain't from these parts." Her voice was as singsongy and twangy as music floating from the log-sided tavern across the street. "And if I had my druthers," she said, pawing at the sidewalk to make her point, "I'd just a' soon stayed where it was warm in Charleston, not here where a dog freezes her hide half the livelong year."

Kito had to step into the circle. "Didn't you hear what she said? *Tundra is missing!* And if our alpha dog is missing, something surely must be wrong."

"Wrong as rain," Schmitty said.

"You mean, 'right as rain'," Chester corrected.

"What could be right about Tundra being gone?"

"Nothing, but the expression is 'right as rain' not 'wrong as—'"

"Enough you two," Kito said. "Tundra is always here, her head high, letting us know that all is well in the village."

"Yuuuup," Gunnar said slowly. "Just—like—our queeeeeen."

"My, oh my," drawled Muffin, "without Tundra, who is gonna lead the dogs in the parade? The celebration is comin' up real soon."

"We'll find her before then," Kito said, taking charge. "Now listen up—we need a plan. If something's wrong, we'll get to the bottom of it more quickly by working together. I propose we form a scouting party."

Chester jumped up and down on his hind legs, springy as a grasshopper. "Right! Just like a 'Neighborhood Watch'," but we could call it . . . Dog Watch! You know—because we dogs keep an eye on things."

"Weeee can work behiiiiind the scenes."

"Well, as Pembrook dogs, we have freedoms that many dogs do not enjoy," Kito said. "And maybe with more freedom comes more responsibility." He'd read that somewhere.

Schmitty, who loved searching through wind-tipped garbage cans, frowned. "You mean we can't have fun anymore?"

"Of course we can still have fun. It's just that," Kito said, "perhaps it's time to go beyond guarding hearth and home. By working together, we could keep the whole village safe—for people *and* dogs." He looked from dog to dog, letting his words sink in. "And right now this is serious. Let me remind you. *Tundra is missing*."

A rare silence hung between them. Kito circled the dogs, something Tundra might have done if she was there. He sat down again, head high. "Dog Watch it is. Who's in? Who will help find Tundra?"

Across Main Street, the tavern door opened, and Gunnar, like a cow turning toward the barn, swung his big head and said, "Gotttttta gooooo," and waddled off to where his sad-eyed begging was rewarded with a steady supply of pretzels and beer sausage.

Muffin's owner, a white-haired woman in pink shorts, stepped from the post office and hopped on her bike. "Muffin, lil' dar-lin'—let's go, sweetie."

Muffin touched noses all around. "Gotta run, y'all." Then she leaped into her owner's arms, took up her seat in the bike basket, and was whisked away toward the beach.

"I'll do what I can," Lucky said, standing on her three legs. "But I need to go home and rest for a bit." She trotted off, quite spryly for a three-legged dog.

Schmitty piped up, smiling wide and wagging his tail until it *thump, thump, thumped* on the fire hydrant. "Hey, I'm in!"

Chester sat square on his haunches and lifted his head, which always made his overbite more prominent. "Ready for anything," he said. "Let's shake down the town."

Kito studied the group. "That makes three—not many, but it's a beginning."

4

Launching Dog Watch

"Now *let's think.*" Kito's back hairs bristled as he paced. "Tundra is the toughest dog in the village, a white German shepherd who doesn't put up with nonsense and holds firmly to the rules of dog behavior. She's always first at the fire hydrant, reminding every dog, teeth-to-neck if necessary, who's the leader, the alpha dog. For her to not show up can only mean trouble."

Chester cocked his head. "Maybe she's out of town with her owner."

"But Mr. Erickson never goes on vacation," Schmitty said.

"True enough," Kito agreed. He looked at the two-story green and white building where Main ended at the lake. The building boasted two signs: Erickson's Very Fine Grocery Store on the left, and on the right, Woody's Fairly Reliable Guide Service. Mr. Erickson was generous with scraps from his butcher's counter, and a dog could always count on Woody for a few fish guts after one of his guided fishing trips. The motto beneath Woody's sign stated: 99 Percent of Our Customers Make It Back to the Dock Alive.

"Maybe Tundra isn't feeling well today," Schmitty said. "She could be sleeping at her home above the store."

"Sick?" Kito replied. "Not Tundra. She's tough as railroad spikes."

Chester tilted his nose skyward, nostrils twitching. "Oh boy—don't get me started! Pork scraps!" And with that, he set off baying.

Kito and Schmitty raced after him and over the tracks to the grocer's shop. Seagulls sent up a racket.

With his white apron tied neatly over his long-sleeved shirt, Mr. Erickson tossed

meat scraps to the birds and dogs—same as he did most mornings. At the nearby docks, boats of all sorts were tied up: fishing boats, sailboats, paddleboats, pontoon boats.

The gulls cried out. One swooped low over Kito's head, startling him. He jumped, but quickly refocused on his mission. He circled wide around the area, looking for anything unusual.

Schmitty blasted like a bullet after a gull, and the bird dropped its chunk of meat and flew off. Smiling, Schmitty snatched the morsel in his teeth.

Chester sat at Mr. Erickson's feet, catching every other scrap.

"Schmitty! Chester!" Kito called. "Did you two forget we're looking for Tundra?"

Chester wagged his tail, not to be guilted.

"Hey, you dogs seen Tundra?" Mr. Erickson asked. He tossed Schmitty a scrap. "Didn't think so," he said to himself, with a shake of his head. "Me either. I'm getting worried. Just not like her. She's always there at the end of my bed sleeping on my feet. Haven't seen tail nor hide of her since yesterday evening. Strange, that's what."

Kito felt the grocer's worry, and on instinct, his fur stood up on edge.

Mr. Erickson gave Kito a sharp look. "Now, now, Kito. You know me. What are you getting your back hairs up about? Quit growling like that."

Kito willed his fur to settle down. He wagged his tail, just to show Mr. Erickson that he really was friendly. "It's not you," he wanted to tell the friendly grocer, "it's the situation."

Mr. Erickson tossed Kito a pork scrap, but Kito missed it. He let a seagull swoop in and steal it from under his nose. He was all jitters. He couldn't concentrate. He couldn't settle down. Not until they found out why their alpha dog—Tundra—was missing.

Heads Up

Just across from Erickson's grocery store, Penny, another golden retriever in town, slept in front of Rainy Day Books. Her owner, Shirley, called out from behind the screen door, "Hi, dogs!"

But the trio—Kito, Chester, and Schmitty—only wagged their tails in reply. Heads high, ears at attention, stomachs full—they had work to do. They rounded Mr. Erickson's building, then trotted past the boathouses and shoreline along Finstad Lane.

"Just like police dogs," Kito said, alert

for anything amiss, "working for peace and justice."

Chester lifted his head even higher, as if trying on a new identity, but the result was that his overbite stuck out farther. He began sniffing the air, then lowered his nose to the ground, where he always did his best investigative work.

"Y'know," Kito said, "Dog Watch feels right to me—as if it's my calling."

"Yeah, why's that?" Schmitty asked.

Kito explained. As an unwanted puppy, he found himself tossed over someone's fence one snowy night. He'd crawled his way to a back door and whimpered. The backdoor opened, and a man brought him to the pound. From there, a woman and two boys took him to their home, only it wasn't a home of love. The mother was always yelling, and one day she left and never returned. Social Services found foster homes for the boys, and he'd ended up back at the pound.

"I whined for the home I knew, bad as it

was—and I was only four months old. That's when Mr. and Mrs. H stepped into my pen. I snarled and cowered, afraid I'd be smacked around like the boys used to do to me, but I remember Mrs. H's words. They were gentle and kind."

"Well, what did she say?" Schmitty asked.

"She said, 'We won't hurt you.' And home I went with them. Took me a long time to trust them—or anybody—but they've been true to their words. Only kindness from them."

"Tear-jerking, Kito," Chester said, rolling his eyes. "I'm touched."

"Well go ahead and joke, but there's too much injustice and cruelty in the world. I know. If we can make our village a safer, more peaceful place, then that's something."

"Yeah," Schmitty added.

Outside Finstad's Motor Repair Shop, old wooden boats sat on large blocks, waiting to be fixed. "Better branch out," Kito said.

The dogs took a three-pronged approach to searching. Chester followed the shoreline and aging docks. Schmitty checked out everything near the brick building. Kito checked around the boats. He thought he caught a hint of Tundra's smell in the long grasses, but decided it was only the scent of a paper grocery bag.

Though he didn't feel terribly brave, he made a good show of it anyway. He nosed around boat tarps, rusted logging chains, and empty crates and barrels. At every stop he kicked at the ground with his hind feet and sent dirt and grass flying. He growled, just to make his presence known. But for all his efforts, the boatyard was eerily quiet.

Schmitty and Chester joined him again on the lane.

"Nothin'" Schmitty said.

"Zip," Chester added. "How 'bout the beach?"

They left the boatyard and rounded a corner to the Pembrook Village Beach. The sign read, NO DOGS ALLOWED, but Kito ignored it. He didn't want to draw attention to his reading ability by making a fuss over rules the other dogs couldn't read. He went with the flow and trotted onto the beach after the others.

Sand nearly burned the pads of his paws.

Three teenagers took turns cannon-balling from the end of the long dock. Mothers visited on blankets, and children played and splashed beside sand castles with turrets, dams, and tiny rivers. A white-haired couple held hands on a bench in the shade of a willow.

"Nothing unusual here," Chester said.

Muffin dashed out from under a beach umbrella. "Hi y'all!" She wagged her stubby tail. "So you big boys got this here Tundra problem figured out?"

"Not yet," Kito said. "But we've just begun."

She scanned the beach. "I've been keepin' my eyes peeled like green grapes for any-thin' might look 'spishus.'"

"You mean 'suspicious'," Chester corrected.

"That's what I said, sweet pea. I'm fixin' to clean out those floppy ears of yours, Chester the Pester. Seems you just ain't hearin' proper these days." With that, she spun away.

At the same moment a little girl with dimply elbows and knees jumped up and left her lavender sand pail in the sand. "Wook! Mommy!" A smile spread across her face, and she pointed at Chester. "Puppy—puppy—puppy!"

"Dog," Chester said under his breath. "I'm a full-grown beagle, not a puppy."

"Oh, that's right. And an AKC beagle at that, don't forget," Kito said, shouldering him.

The girl ran and stumbled and ran again—straight for Chester—whipping up a tiny tornado of sand as she approached.

6

A Troubling Clue

Chester braced himself as the little girl whirled toward him. "Hey, I don't mind being petted, but if she intends to haul me around like a stuffed toy or a doll, I'm outta here."

"At least she thinks you're cute," said Kito.

"Hey, watch this—Schmitty to the rescue!" The black Lab darted across the girl's path, threw himself down at her feet, rolled on his back, then head to his paws, he wagged his tail like crazy.

"Oh, woo my fend?" The girl giggled. "Mommy! He wikes me!" She toddled on chubby legs after Schmitty as he made his way to the girl's mother, who happened to be seated at a picnic table with a spread of food. Schmitty parked his rump down, as if pledging his loyalty to them for life. Tongue hanging, tail flapping, he smiled as wide as his pink mouth could stretch.

"Aren't you a sweet fellow?" the mother said. "You're the friendliest dog in Pembrook, aren't you? Need a treat?"

Schmitty wagged his tail harder and sent sand flying.

The woman reached for a half-nibbled sandwich. "Just happened to have a leftover roast beef—here y'go."

Oh so gently, Schmitty leaned toward the sandwich and took it from the woman's outstretched hand. He gulped it whole and waited for more.

She held up her hands. "That's all."

Then Schmitty dashed back to Kito and Chester. "That, my fine furry friends, is how it's done. See how easy?"

Kito wasn't amused. Their mission was

going nowhere in a hurry. "Yeah, if you don't care about looking for Tundra."

Schmitty's black tail dropped slightly. "Oh, that's right, I nearly forgot."

"You mean," Chester said, "you did forget. Went completely out of that cute empty head of yours."

"Hey, you had your chance. You're jealous you didn't get the sandwich, and it was meaty."

"I have my dignity, not like some garbage hounds—"

Schmitty nipped at Chester's front legs and Chester caught Schmitty's tail in his teeth. Soon they were tumbling and rolling in a cloud of sand.

"Hey!" Kito said, pushing his way into the fight. "You two get along! Either we're a team or we're nothing." He stared both of them down—a stern growl rumbling in his throat—until they stopped. "Got it?"

Chester and Schmitty touched noses, then raced each other along the sandy beach. Kito followed behind, weaving around sun bathers. He exhaled hard. He had hoped they'd find a trace of Tundra by now. He needed her back. Already he had grown tired of the role of alpha dog. It was work.

At the edge of the village, they stopped and turned around at a sign that read, Welcome to Pembrook—Population: 199.

"They should really count the dogs when they figure the population for that sign," Kito said. He looked to the dogs, almost forgetting himself.

Schmitty and Chester looked at him, waiting for more.

"I'm just saying—I've heard people talk and they say that sign says the population is a hundred ninety-nine in this village, but how many dogs do you think live here?"

"Twenty?" Chester ventured.

"Thirty?" Schmitty guessed.

"Nineteen by my last count," Kito said. "To be fair, seems the sign should read, 'People: a hundred ninety-nine, Dogs: nineteen, Cats: don't bother, Chipmunks: a zillion.'"

"Yeah, but what if the dog count is down

to eighteen?" Schmitty studied the ground, head down. "What if Tundra—"

With his teeth Kito tugged lightly at Schmitty's ear. "Hey, we can't think that way. Be positive. Upbeat. Hope for the best. Dog Watch has to be built on hope, not despair."

"You make a sharp point," Chester said. "So let's get back on the case."

They hurried along the shoreline, past Erickson's Very Fine Grocery Store and Woody's Fairly Reliable Guide Service, past the Wharf Ice-Cream Shop, the squat train depot, and over the railroad tracks.

Chester took off, nose to the ground. *Snuffle, snuffle, snuffle!* "Criminy crackers! Something over here!" He was in hot pursuit, winding around oak trees at the tiny park by the water. Nearly breathing in the dirt itself, he kept on the scent.

Kito trotted alongside him, his nose never as keen as Chester's. He hadn't picked up the scent of anything yet. "Don't tell me it's hot dogs again, or the drippings from another ice-cream cone."

"Tundra—*snuffle, snuffle, snuff, snuff*—was here. *Snuffle, snuffle*—sure as a shingle!"

Schmitty bounded ahead, weaving back and forth like a snake over the whole park. "He's right. Now I'm picking up the scent too. She was here, but how long ago?"

From Seven Oaks Park, just below where the tracks crossed the lift bridge into Pembrook, Kito could see his home across the bay. Mr. and Mrs. H were mere dots sitting on the dock, fishing and reading—their favorite pastimes.

"This way," Chester said, nose pressed into the earth. He raced up the railroad embankment to the tracks again.

Glancing toward the lift bridge and then beyond the depot, Kito double-checked to make sure no trains were coming. They didn't need to lose members of Dog Watch to a train accident. The coast was clear.

Chester zigzagged closer and closer to the steel rails. Then he slowed and began a more in-depth, inch-by-inch search of the gravel between the wood railroad ties.

Schmitty whined, then turned to Kito. "You thinkin' what I'm thinkin'? She got hit by a train, didn't she?"

The sun burned hot, ripening the thick smells of engine diesel and the creosote in the railroad ties. Kito didn't answer.

Finally Chester stopped and sat on his haunches, facing the other two. "From what I can decipher, she was in the park, made her way up here to the train tracks . . . but her scent ends—here."

"I knew it!" Schmitty wailed, rushing forward and flopping down beside Chester. "A train hit her, poor girl!"

"Uh, hang on pal," Chester said. "I don't think so. Quit your sniveling. From what I can piece together, she must have *disappeared* from this spot."

Schmitty whined all the more loudly. "Don't you see? Someone picked up her poor body and disposed of it, not even bothering to let Mr. Erickson know! Not so much as a decent burial!"

Kito examined the spot where Chester

claimed Tundra had disappeared. "No sign of death. You can always smell it, and it's nowhere near here—thank goodness."

Schmitty shook his head and flopped his ears. "Then I don't get it. She just vanished? Maybe . . . I saw a TV show on UFOs . . . maybe one came down and some alien picked her up, being she's our alpha dog, maybe she was needed on another planet. . . ."

Chester tilted his head. "Too much TV fries your brains; haven't you heard our owners say that? Seems to me she went from this spot right up into a boxcar."

Kito considered Chester's words. "But why would she take off? She wouldn't go off on her own. She's true-blue to the rest of us."

"Where is she vulnerable?" Chester asked. "What are her weaknesses? How could she be lured into going anywhere?"

"Ah," Schmitty said. "Now I see where you're going. Rawhide bones? Chewy sticks?"

"Now your brain's barkin'!" Chester said.

"I'm thinking Meaty Beefy Bone Nuggets? Her paws-down favorite?"

"You're right there," Kito said. "Nothing gets her drooling like Meaty Beefies . . . and she sorta loses her head when food's around. Yet she takes her job of alpha dog too seriously to run off. Tundra's strong and smart, but with her weakness for food, she might have been lured into a boxcar and whisked away."

The dogs touched noses in agreement. As they gazed down the tracks, their back hairs shot up like porcupine quills.

7

Vandal in the Village

"**We have to** go after her!" Schmitty barked.

"Not so fast," Kito said. "Follow me." He scampered down the grassy embankment, tail curved over his back, and flopped in the shade of a towering oak.

Chester stood over Kito, glowering. "Slobbery spit! What are you doing? Don't you care about Tundra? We have no time to waste—and you're doing what? Crashing in the grass? Snoozing? What's come over you?"

"We must think before we act," Kito answered. "For all we know, the railroad tracks stretch both ways forever."

He let those words sink in. Dog Watch was a mission-in-progress. He might be faster at putting things together and forming plans, but he needed to respect the time other dogs needed to absorb new information. If they were going to be a team, they had to act like one.

Chester looked up at the tracks and toward the depot. Schmitty followed his gaze.

"And if we set out," Kito continued, "which way would we head?"

"North to Canada," said Chester. "Tundra doesn't like the heat. It would be cooler up there."

"No," Schmitty said. "South through Minnesota and the States, because—oh, I don't know. I'm just not agreeing with Chester."

"Exactly. That's why we're stopping to think. We could take off and be going in the wrong direction. For all we know, Tundra might still be riding the rails. She could be hundreds, thousands of miles away. There's no way we're going to catch up to her by walking."

Chester and Schmitty stared at each other, dumbstruck.

Kito rose and trotted to the shore for a drink of cold water. "Besides, on a day like this," he said between lapping, "no sense in chasing harebrained after her—the heat could dry us into leather chews." He returned to the cool grass in the shade and stretched out.

The other two flopped down too. Schmitty rolled, scratching his back on scattered twigs and rocks. Chester stretched out, legs and paws skyward. "Hey," he said. "The banner was pulled down last night—right?"

"Yup."

"Right."

"And Mr. Erickson said Tundra hadn't shown up last night. Two odd events in one evening in our little village. More than a coincidence, wouldn't you agree?"

"You bet," Schmitty said.

"Possibly," Kito replied. Although it was too early to draw solid conclusions, anything was possible at this point. He sprang to his legs. "Okay, rest time is over. Let's check for fresh news at the hydrant."

Up Duluth Street the dogs trotted, back on patrol. They crossed Main to the hydrant.

"No news," Chester said, sniffing for the latest news, "but plenty of worry goin' round. Dogs are upset, that's what."

Just then Gunnar waddled out from the shady side of the tavern.

Kito knew better than to laugh at Gunnar's looks. Loose folds of skin hung around his neck and chest like a baggy sweater. But basset hounds were great trackers, and all that extra skin, dewlap, and long ears were meant to hold the scent of game that Englishmen hunted. Hard to imagine a pack of baying beagles, but a pack of baying basset hounds . . .

Gunnar blinked his saggy eyelids, looking like he just woke up. "I've been keeeeepin' an eye ooopen for trouuuuble." His long floppy ears and drooling jowls nearly touched his front feet.

"In your dreams," Chester said. "I saw you snoozin' back there. You can't fool me."

Gunnar frowned and chased Chester around the hydrant—about five strides—and stopped, breathing heavily. "Sheeeesh! Gotta sloooow down in this heat."

"Good idea," said Schmitty, snickering. "Don't move too fast, old pal. Someone could have a heart attack if they saw you speeding."

"Ooooh, knock it—off." Gunnar shook his head and droplets of drool splattered the post office steps.

"Let's get serious!" Kito said. "We need every dog in the village if Dog Watch is going to work. Gunnar knows the tavern—who comes and goes, who lingers latest, who cuts outside for a smoke. Gunnar, you know a whole lot about what happens on the night side of life better than any dog around."

"Yup, that's truuuuue."

"Last night did you see anything unusual, anything out of the ordinary?"

"Uhh, noope."

"Think harder."

"Well, maaaaybe a few motorcyclists, some fiiiiiishermen bragging 'bout their fish. But moooostly—just regulars. Eeeverybody seeeeemed plennnnty nice."

"That's 'cause they fed you," Chester said. "Of course there are going to be new faces. With the celebration coming at us like a freight train, we're going to have an increasing stream of tourists and relatives filling up the village. Going to be one big party soon."

"Exactly what I'm afraid of," Kito said. "It's going to be mighty difficult to—"

Just then the fire hydrant hummed. A fine mist sprayed from its seal. In seconds the mist turned to streams and sprayed the dogs in their eyes.

Kito's ears flattened. He jumped back,

out of the water, but kept his eyes on the hydrant. "Better let Mr. Cutler know. Don't want this thing to flood Main Street!" And at that, Kito sat on his haunches, inhaled to full lung capacity, and sent up a volley of barks. Chester joined in with his high-pitched baying, Schmitty yapped, and Gunnar added his baritone bellowing bark.

Within moments Mr. Cutler stormed out of the community building's attached garage, rounded the corner, and looked their way. A tiny rainbow formed in the hydrant's mist.

With a look of dismay, Mr. Cutler ran to his tool shed, then sprinted to the corner of Main with tools in hand—ready to help.

8

Mavis, the Postmaster

Before Mr. Cutler reached the corner, Mavis, the Postmaster, flew out of the post office's door. "What in Sam's name is going on out here? What in the world could be—" But when she saw the leaking hydrant, she jumped back—but not before her gray-blue uniform got wet.

Within seconds Mr. Cutler plowed through the spraying water, fastened a large wrench around the top of the hydrant, and cranked it with all his might. The hydrant quieted. He took off his cap, shook it out, then wiped droplets from his forehead. "Whew! Guess I better have the fire department take a look at this one."

"Yes, you had better," Mavis said, her white hair sternly combed behind her ears. She waved her pointer finger, the nail yellowed from smoking. "The mail must go through—and a water leak at my front steps would shut me down."

"You're sure in a sour mood, Mavis. What did you eat for breakfast? A bowl of crab apples? How 'bout 'thank you very kindly, Mr. Cutler' or some such?"

"My mood is my business," she replied. In gray postal shorts, she stood with her muscular legs spaced a foot apart, her arms crossed. "For your information, the mail quadruples this time of year with tourists returning to their lake cabins and visiting the area. It isn't easy getting the mail sorted in a timely manner every day. Last thing I need is a disaster at my doorstep."

"Oh, you'd make sure the mail got through even if there was a flood," Mr. Cutler teased. "You're the hardest-working person in town, and hardest headed, too."

And it was probably true. Mavis had the steely will of a beaver. She made sure the mail was sorted and ready for pick up by 10:00 a.m., sharp. But if anyone asked for their mail two minutes before ten, the dogs outside could hear Mavis's special brand of customer service: "You think you're special or something? You'll wait like everyone else. Ten o'clock, not a minute sooner." Anyone who stayed on in the village learned not to cross Mavis about her mail routines.

Kito sat a few feet from her. The postmaster reminded him of Tundra—another alpha female. The day Tundra had pinned Schmitty to the ground, Mavis yanked Tundra off Schmitty's neck. "No fighting!" Mavis had commanded. "Tundra, *sit!*" And Tundra—likely humiliated to her core—reluctantly obeyed. From that day on, when Mavis closed the post office for her lunch break and sat outside on the bench, Tundra always came by to put her head in Mavis's lap.

Despite Mavis's gruffness, every evening, from the windows of her tiny home only half a block away, her lovely violin music floated from her windows. She wasn't the type of person to cause trouble for Tundra or the village parade. But when it came to dogs, she was always the first to scold them if they were out of line.

"And what are you starin' at?" she said, meeting Kito's eyes. Then she turned on her tennis-shoe heels and snapped the door shut behind her.

Mr. Cutler closed his toolbox and whistled "When the Saints Go Marching In" as he headed past the community building's flagpole to the garage.

"Good old handy dandy Mr. Cutler," Chester said.

"Yup," Schmitty agreed, "he's like the village that holds the glue together."

"You mean the glue that holds the village together."

"Yeah, whatever."

Suddenly Kito squinted at the hydrant

and circled it. "Look! These nicks weren't here this morning! I think someone was up to no good. . . . Someone loosened the large washer on this hydrant and tampered with public property."

"Yeah, same person who was messing with the banner, I'll bet," Chester added.

"Who was up to no good with Tundra," Schmitty continued. "And we're going to find out who that someone is—after I head home for a bite to eat. Missed breakfast."

"But you ate at the beach," Chester said, going nose to nose with Schmitty.

"Doesn't matter," said Kito. "We should all head home and check in. This is not the time to make our families worry about us. Then they might lock us at home. We must hold to our routines. Maintain our usual habits of eating, sleeping, napping. Home for a bit, then out the door, and back on the case again."

9

The Smell of Trouble

When the dogs returned home, Mr. and Mrs. H were standing on the end of the dock beside their idling wooden boat. Mr. H shouted out, "Hey, boys! You're just in time. Let's go!"

Kito pushed away concerns about not being around for Dog Watch patrol and wagged his tail. He loved a good boat ride, wind in his face, especially on a hot afternoon. He hopped in the front, behind the windshield, and sat between Mr. and Mrs. H. Chester ducked under the enclosed bow to sleep on top of extra seat cushions. Off they went, motor roaring, leaving behind a white ruffle of water.

"We're gonna catch some fish today," Mr. H proclaimed.

Kito winced. He wouldn't have minded a short boat ride, but fishing with Mr. H meant hours at a stretch. He was a fisherman who didn't give up easily, even though he rarely caught anything.

By late afternoon, Mr. H had caught a northern. "We're on a roll, darlin'. We could keep going, break our record!"

Mrs. H's line arced. She reeled in a foot-long walleye. "Two fish!" She laughed. "Now we have enough for dinner."

Kito barked in agreement as Mr. H netted the fish. He shot Chester a hopeful look. Now they'd head back. Good.

"Honey," he said, "I can't think of a better way to celebrate our thirtieth anniversary. Kids gone. Time for fishing—time together."

Chester snorted.

They motored toward a peninsula with a

tiny sand beach and cluster of cedar trees. Mr. and Mrs. H stretched out a blanket, opened a bottle of sparkling cranberry juice, and built a small campfire near shore.

After a swim in the lake, tug-of-war over a stick, and a game of "You're It," Kito and Chester rested on the sand.

"Nothing like a shore supper," Mr. H proclaimed, frying battered fillets.

"Oh, I almost forgot," said Mrs. H as she emptied a plastic bag of dog food onto a plate and set it before the dogs. "Dig in."

When they finished eating, they stretched on the sand, their noses aimed at the boat. Kito counted the minutes until they could return to their true mission.

"We barely got Dog Watch launched," Chester whined. "By now the other dogs will think we've bailed out."

"I know, but what can we do?"

Before long, mosquitoes began buzzing. The Hollinghorsts packed up their picnic gear, snuffed out their fire, and boated back. The setting sun left the sky plum-orange-red.

When the boat touched the dock, Kito said, "Let's take off quick."

"Right-o."

They sprang from the boat and darted toward the woodpile at the edge of the yard. They pretended to be searching for chipmunks, but gradually slipped away toward the shadows.

"Uh, guys?" Mr. H called. "Come! It's late. Time to turn in."

Their tails dropped low, and they stopped, turned, and reluctantly ambled toward their owners and the house.

Kito curled up on his cedar-filled dog bed, while Chester, always the baby, stretched out on the end of Mr. and Mrs. H's bed. It was just as well; Chester and Mr. H were evenly matched at snoring, and a little distance from them was just fine.

From the corner of the bedroom, he noticed the book Mrs. H had been reading in bed. The spine read *Gone with the Wind.* The words lingered in his mind. That was exactly what had happened to Tundra. Even with worries, all that fresh lake air sent Kito into a deep, heavy, all-night slumber.

Next morning he awakened to the sound of different vehicles moving somewhere beyond his home. He lifted his head, sniffing. Different smells of truck and car exhaust. *Strangers.* He flinched.

Chester awakened too, rudely falling off

the bed onto the wood floor. But as soon as he hit, he was on his feet. "We've overslept! We're supposed to be on patrol. Some lead dog you are," he ranted, standing over Kito. "I was relying on you to get us going by now. Tundra could be at the Arctic Circle or Florida by now. And what are we doing? Sleeping in!"

Kito heaved himself out of his bed. "Hey, same as you, buddy." And at that moment, two thoughts collided: Tundra and the festival. Tundra always led the Pembrook dogs behind the mayor's car in the parade down Main Street. Whoever had tampered with the banner and hydrant was tampering with the parade by getting Tundra out of town. Without her, the other dogs would barely know where to line up, let alone stay in line for the whole parade.

Kito stretched, headed to the door, and scratched. Mr. H set down the newspaper and his coffee cup at the kitchen table and opened the door. "Thought you boys were going to sleep forever. Big day tomorrow with the festival. Hope you can handle the commotion, Kito. Last year—"

But before Mr. H could continue, Kito and Chester darted outside and ran out of the yard, back on the job.

10

Mistaken Identity

This morning the normally sleepy village bustled with commotion. Kito and Chester trotted past the tennis courts to the community building. "Morning, Kito . . . Chester," Mr. Cutler called, busily hammering together a platform. A sign on the ground said DUNKING BOOTH.

The dogs moved on and wove through stands and camper trailers. Vendors were busily unpacking boxes and setting up their makeshift booths for the next day's big event. One man was unpacking velvet paintings of horses, dogs, and Elvis. The sign above a food stand said Wanita's BBQ Turkey Drumsticks, but Kito couldn't smell them cooking yet. Just thinking of all the food that would soon be around, he began to drool. Plenty of leftovers would be ready for finding, if a dog was attentive.

A pair of motorcycles, their engines reeking of dust and hot fuel, rested outside the tavern. Kito didn't like motorcycles. They were too noisy, and their owners drove them too fast down Main Street. Last year he'd nearly been run over by one as he crossed to the post office.

Village dogs crowded around the hydrant, all yapping at once.

Muffin stood on her hind legs and placed her tiny front feet on top of the hydrant.

"I mean, breakin' news," Muffin said.

Kito and Chester joined the group just as the other dogs quieted.

"At the beach yesterday," Muffin continued, now that she had their full attention, "kids were talkin' 'bout Tundra. One boy claimed he saw her wanderin' in the woods and that wolves got her. But then another said, 'No, you're lying' 'cause he said he saw her stuck in a bear trap. What do y'all think, anything to it?"

"Nothing but stories," Kito said with a nod toward the train tracks. "Yesterday, after we left the beach, Chester picked up Tundra's scent at the tracks. It disappeared right where a dog could hop a boxcar—or be forced onto one. I believe she ended up on a train outta here."

"How?" Muffin asked, her little round eyes wider than usual.

"We don't know."

"Where?" asked Lucky.

"We don't know that either."

"Oh, I'm fit to be tied with worry!" Muffin cried.

"Don't worry your little head, Muffin," Chester said.

"And don't worry your little pea brain, either," she replied with a yip.

Kito took charge. "Remember, there are

no dumb ideas, no stupid questions, no small notions in Dog Watch." He looked around sternly at Muffin, Gunnar, Schmitty, Lucky, and Chester.

"This morning we need every able dog to make the rounds, to stay alert. If we can figure out who is trying to spoil our village celebration, then maybe we'll find who is behind putting Tundra on a train. My gut tells me the two are connected."

Kito paused for effect.

The dogs stood motionless.

"By tomorrow this street will be packed," he continued. "Today's the day to make progress. Teamwork! That's what we need!"

Kito could hardly believe himself. Though he preferred staying in the background, he was proving he could lead when he had to.

Lucky lifted her head high. "A loss of a leg doesn't change who I am. It's meant a few adjustments getting around, but I can still run—a little slower, perhaps—but I'm still the same dog. I'll pull my weight right along with the rest of you."

"You got what it takes, Lucky," Chester said, nudging his snout under her muzzle.

Halfway down the street at the edge of the curb, a quarrel broke out between a man and a woman. The dogs swung their heads toward the commotion and looked on.

Under the canvas awning and sign for Jojo's Jiffy Jewelry stood a lavender-haired woman. Twice the size of the mustached man from the neighboring Popcorn Palace booth, she was yelling at him until her face matched the color of her red floral blouse.

"Check it out," Kito said, and the dogs raced off together. They fanned out behind the booths, got caught up in the noise, and began barking.

"I need good lighting at my booth!" the woman hollered. "How will my customers put beads together if they can't see what they're doing? How will I get set up today? It's shady under here and I can barely see a thing!"

"Hey, you act as if I did something," said the man as he straightened his gold necklace.

"The power keeps going off. I think

you're unplugging my extension cord. Some kind of prank, right? Well I—"

The dogs pressed closer.

"Give me a break, lady. I just got here and already I have a splitting headache, so please, no screaming. I didn't mess with your cord. I've had to plug mine back in twice already this morning. You think you have troubles."

Kito stepped to the back of Jojo's booth and bristled. Someone in brown overalls was suspiciously hunched over a coil of blue electrical cord. Kito growled under his breath. The culprit!

A rush of fear and adrenaline flooded through his four legs. But he wouldn't run. He'd catch this man red-handed. He snarled and bared his teeth, and as the man spun, Kito nipped at the man's outstretched hand.

Only—it wasn't a stranger—it was Mr. Cutler.

Mr. Cutler jumped back, holding his hand. "Kito. What's with you? You nipped me?" He looked at his hand. "No blood, thank goodness."

Kito sat back, then flopped on the ground and rolled on his back subserviently. He'd just made a big, stupid, embarrassing mistake. "I'm sorry," he said, but of course, Mr. Cutler couldn't hear his words.

Just then Jojo and the popcorn man rounded the corner, trailed by several dogs.

Kito felt humiliated. His fear was his worst enemy sometimes. It clouded his senses—made him leap before he looked. Mr. Cutler of all people!

"Now what's going on?" Jojo asked.

"Heard you were having problems with your extension cords," explained Mr. Cutler. "Came over to help. Just plugged your cord back in. Think the dogs have been tripping over your cords?"

"I don't know what to think," she said flatly. "This just better not happen tomorrow, that's all I can say."

"Oh, I'll keep things in order, don't you worry none."

"Well, thank you." She glanced back at her booth. "Lights are on, that's all I care about." Then she held out her hand to the popcorn man. "I'm sorry," she said. "Let's start over. I'm Jojo and you're—"

"Pete."

"And I'm sorry too," Mr. Cutler said, looking at Kito. "But I'm going to have to report you to Mrs. Burkowski—and notify your owners. Can't have you nipping at people, especially with the big celebration tomorrow."

Life was strange. Just moments ago Kito had been feeling pretty good about leading in Tundra's absence. Now he'd mistaken Mr. Cutler for a stranger and was to be reported. That meant one more round sticker on his page in the *DOGGY MUG SHOTS* book. A sticker! He hung his head. He wanted nothing more than to dig a big hole in the ground, crawl in, and bury himself like a dog bone.

11

Grounded

"How could you?" Chester said, flopping on the sofa beside Kito. "How could you nip Mr. Cutler? He's always good to us."

"New overalls."

"New overalls? I don't—"

"He was wearing brand-new overalls, not his usual faded tan ones. They smelled new—different—and I . . . well, it threw me."

"Huh. And lucky me. You get grounded and I'm told I have to stay home and keep you company. This is just a peachy situation, that's what."

69

"Now, not that I want to risk another sticker, but I have an idea."

"Do I want to hear it? I mean, look at us. Some Dog Watch we got going, right?"

"Listen, Mr. H is busy writing his latest novel, and Mrs. H. is hanging paintings in the community building for tomorrow's art show. They're artists, Chester. They get lost in their work. Think they're really going to keep a close eye on us every minute?"

"I see where this is going."

"We'll just cut out for a short look around."

They rose to their feet, shook their coats, and headed to the door. Chester whined and Kito barked. Before long, Mr. H started down the spiral wood staircase from his studio, one hand on the rail and the other reading a letter from an editor. "Okay, okay," he said, absentmindedly letting them out, completely forgetting about Kito's grounding.

"It's not like we're disobeying," Kito said. "Not exactly. I mean, we're dogs, right? He let us out. Far as Mr. and Mrs. H know, we don't understand we're grounded. And they're the keepers of the door and their dogs, right?"

"Yeah, I guess that makes sense," Chester said. "But we better make sure we steer clear of trouble. If you get reported for anything else, you could be grounded forever."

"Let's keep a low profile, then. The village and Tundra depend on us."

The two touched noses in agreement, then stepped onto Pine Street, the air sweet with blossoms. The sky was tinged rosy-orange as the sun went down. Nearly time for the nightly news at 10:00 and it was still light outside. First the dogs cut through yards, avoiding streets, and peered inside the community building windows. Mrs. H was there with some other people, hammer and wires in hand, covering the walls with local artists' work. But dozens of paintings were already hung, and Kito guessed that Mrs. H would be finished and returning home before long.

They had a little time, but not much. In

the dusky light, they trotted to the booths.

Kito sniffed around. Motorcycle fumes raised his back hairs. Perhaps a stranger rode in on a motorcycle and started trouble, from tampering with the fire hydrant to messing with the electrical cords.

Music, laughter, and voices spilled from the tavern as Kito and Chester crept around the back of the building. Ripened garbage in cans permeated the hot, humid night air.

"Mmmmm," Chester said, "smells good."

"Yeah, but if you start garbage-can diving, you'll have a stomachache. You weren't *bred* for garbage food, remember?" Kito had too many unforgettable memories of when his buddy's stomach gave way.

"Hi, guys," Gunnar said, ambling toward them. "Smelled soooomething rotten back heeeeere, then I fiiiigured it waaaaas you two." He grinned at his own joke.

"Funny. We're hoping to dig up more clues," Chester said. "But on the sly, as Kito is supposed to be at home in lockdown."

"Thaaaaat's what I heard." Gunnar lifted his heavy head and stared at Kito. "Neeever thought yooooou would get looockdown."

"He goofed up, big-time," Chester said. "So have you come up with anything?"

"Ooooh, I been sleeeeepin' off toooo many Slim Jims. A guy rolled in on a Haaaarley, then came inside. Fed meeee till I could baaarely move."

Chester and Kito exchanged glances.

"Harley motorcycle? Yesterday, you say?" Chester asked.

Gunnar nodded, his eyes droopier than usual.

"About what time?" Kito asked. "Mid-morning, perhaps?"

"Maaybe, maaaybe not. It's dark moost of the time in there."

"I've caught the whiff of motorcycle fumes near the hydrant and the booths. For now, this may be just the lead we need. Thanks for your help."

"Noooo problem."

As the lights went out at the community building, Kito and Chester bolted home, whined at the door, and Mr. H let them inside. He padded back up to his studio. The dogs followed up after him. By the time the front door handle turned and Mrs. H stepped in, Kito and Chester had settled themselves comfortably next to Mr. H's sheepskin slippers.

12

Parade Disaster

That night Kito's dreams turned dark. He slept fitfully. On a craggy mountain, her eyes wild with terror, stood Tundra. Beneath her the mountain rumbled and moved, and when she sat down, she began slipping and was forced to claw her way back to the mountain's peak. From across a wide river, Kito watched—helpless—unable to get across, unable to stop her from sliding down to a dangerous, bottomless depth. He tried with all his might to leap the river, and with a violent kick of his back legs, he woke up, shivering and panting. His stomach churned with worry.

Chester was snoring at the foot of Mr. and Mrs. H's bed.

Kito closed his eyes and tried to go back to sleep. But his dream had left him rattled. What did it mean? More than ever he worried for Tundra's well-being.

He finally stood, rose from his corduroy dog bed, and gazed out the window. The moon lit the bay and water danced in its silver-white beam. Having Tundra missing reminded him that life was short and uncertain. The only certain thing was to be a good friend to the end of one's days. And to not lose hope.

Chester woke, slipped from the bed, and came to his side. "I can't sleep either. What's cookin'?"

"Worrying."

"Me too."

"I had a bad dream—about Tundra."

"Yeah. Two days since she disappeared. Not good."

Kito touched noses with Chester. "Let's try and snatch a few more winks. Whoever is causing trouble hasn't been caught yet . . . and I'm not giving up on Tundra, not by a long shot."

Kito clawed and dug at his bed until the lumpiness was just so, then he dropped down into a fluffy ball and eventually slept.

The coffeemaker's *drip-drip*ping woke the dogs.

Chester leaped from the bed. "Ready?"

Kito's dream still clung to him like rain-soaked fur. But he pushed away his fears. "Ready."

Then he strode for the door, whined, and Mr. H let them out. "No trouble today, Kito. You be good or you'll be locked in the garage, got it?"

He and Chester made their normal rounds, checked the dock, marked the yard's perimeter, then headed straight for the middle of Pembrook. Breakfast could wait.

The Pembrook Celebration banner floated

proudly over Main Street, undisturbed by vandals this time.

A dozen vendors, including Pete and Jojo, chatted at one of several picnic tables set up on the lawn outside the community building. "Weather's lookin' good," said one.

"Couldn't be better!"

"Sky is blue as blue can be."

Within hours the village would be charged as if struck by lightning. Already the smell of *strangers* was in the air. Kito hoped he could survive the day without a sticker. He was lucky—his time-out had lasted just under a day. It could have been much longer. Mr. H had explained that if he had actually broken the skin on Mr. Cutler's hand, he would have earned another sticker. As it turned out, Mr. H had received a warning call instead.

Lucky and Muffin were pacing at the fire hydrant, along with Schmitty and Gunnar.

"How can we be in the parade without Tundra?" Lucky was saying.

Muffin shook out her curly coat. "We'll

be a sorry mess without her, sugar."

Kito and Chester joined them.

The dogs shared what they had found: dead-end leads, tips that turned out to be unfounded, rumors that proved to be untrue.

"No matter. All dogs on high alert today," Kito reminded them. "If anyone has foul plans in mind, today is the day they'll take things a step further."

After heading home for a shared bowl of Hearty Hound and a good round of scratching, Kito and Chester walked with Mr. and Mrs. H to the midmorning festivities.

Aromas from popcorn, hot dogs, cotton candy, caramel apples, minidonuts, barbecued-ribs-on-a-stick mingled in the air. "It's enough to make me drool," Chester said, tail wagging.

A skinny, wire-haired man hobbled on stilts along Main Street.

Kito darted sideways, alarmed at the man's height and his tottering way of walking. Things were downright scary.

"It's okay, Kito," said Mrs. H, stroking

his back. "No need to get worried."

Two draft horses pulled a straw-filled wagon. On the side hung a sign: Rides—50 Cents! Kito crossed the street to avoid the massive hooves and nearly dashed into a moving motorcycle.

The Harley carried a man and woman— matching black leather pants, dusty boots, and belly-tight vests—and headed toward the village beach. Kito bristled, certain those cycle fumes meant trouble.

When Mr. and Mrs. H stopped by the John Deere tractor booth, the dogs veered off. Chester snuffled as they scouted around. Kito's stomach felt as knotted and frayed as a puppy-chewed rope toy.

Mr. Jorgenson, the village mayor, visited with the crowd, shaking hands and kissing the foreheads of babies.

He stood on the deck of the community building, put a yellow megaphone to his mouth, and called, "Parade lineup in ten minutes at Pembrook Park!"The mayor was short and round, and his bald head glistened like aluminum foil. Today he was all smiles.

Kito mused at how people practiced leadership. No teeth to the neck to make a point. Instead, people at village council meetings shouted and argued until Mayor Jorgenson pounded his wooden gavel. Though people were different, sometimes they got in their own sort of dog fights.

Kito and Chester trotted after the mayor to Pembrook Park. Parade participants and dogs lined up behind the mayor's light blue pickup truck.

The mayor's silver-haired mother sat behind the steering wheel, barely visible. Tiny Mrs. Jorgenson drove her son everywhere. He'd spent so many years studying psychology at college that he apparently never learned how to drive. Standing in the back of the truck, the mayor held up a huge box of Chunky Bites dog treats. "Ready, dogs?"

A dozen dogs had already arrived, with more drifting in. The dogs jumped up toward the box, falling over one another.

Kito pushed to the front and faced the dogs. "Line up," he said. "Settle down. We can do this, even if Tundra can't be here today. She'd insist we behave."

The dogs settled down. Kito was relieved. He didn't want to be challenged and have to have an all-out dogfight to prove his point. "You know the routine. As long as you follow the truck without fighting, you'll get treats."

Behind the dogs a line formed with antique cars, a marching band, go-carts, bagpipe players, powwow dancers, and floats of all kinds. The line curved around the park's perimeter like a Chinese dragon. Never had the park slides, swings, and playground equipment looked so empty.

Wonk! Wonk! Mrs. Jorgenson sounded the horn. "Noon!" she called. "Let's get Baby rolling!" Baby was what she always called her truck.

"Let the Pembrook Parade begin!" shouted the mayor.

Clapping and shouting erupted, cars honked, and the mayor's mother started the truck engine. But the moment it pulled forward, the pickup *thumped, clumped, bumped*—and stopped!

Mayor Jorgenson lost his balance, stumbled, and spilled the dog biscuits. Half of the biscuits fell into the truckbed, but the rest fell on the ground.

The dogs dog-piled into one another. Kito clanked his front teeth on the truck's silver bumper. Chester tripped and fell. Other dogs piled up and started wrestling.

"Oh dear!" cried Mrs. Jorgenson, patting her face with a handkerchief. Mayor Jorgenson's head glistened with sweat as he hurriedly picked up biscuits.

"Quit puuuushing!" Gunnar complained.

"That wasn't me, sugar!" Muffin cried.

"Hey, he started it!" yelled another dog.

The mayor jumped out of the truck. He talked into his megaphone. "Now, don't worry, we'll be under way in just a minute." Then he and his mother circled the truck, checking every tire until they stopped at the truck's right front wheel.

"Oh dear!" said Mrs. Jorgenson.

The mayor's face lost its usual cheeriness and turned from light pink to tomato red. "Why—someone has slashed Baby's tire!"

13

Hopes Slashed

Villagers left their places in line and rushed to look at the mayor's tire.

"Now we'll have to wait to get it fixed!" a man complained.

"And it's getting hot. We can't wait around—"

"Could take an hour or more," said another.

The mayor climbed onto the back of his truck and stood facing the crowd. "No need to worry," he said. "Someone was up to no good, that's clear. But the parade must go on, and there's no reason we can't proceed as usual."

"But I'll ruin Baby's silver rims!" cried Mrs. Jorgenson.

"No, Mother," he said, jumping down from the truck again. "You come with me, and we'll have a fine walk down Main Street." He smiled and held out his arm for her to take.

"No thanks, dear. I'll wait here with Baby and keep an eye on her. You go ahead."

With that, the mayor marched ahead, holding the box of Chunky Bites dog treats in one hand, and with the other, tossing the prized snacks over his shoulder. The Pembrook dogs followed the mayor, with Kito at the head of them, keeping order in the dogs' current state of emergency.

The band played. The tuba boomed and clarinets shrieked. The antique cars honked their horns.

"Let's not get too close," the band conductor called to his students. "The dogs need room to catch biscuits."

At the head of the band, three baton twirlers in purple skirts and gold tops threw batons high, spun around, and caught them again. Kito was amazed. He could barely catch a biscuit in his mouth.

He turned to Schmitty. "So what do you make of the slashed tire? Another parade disaster, wouldn't you say?"

"Yup."

"But who? That's what rattles me."

Schmitty's eyes were focused on the Chunky Bites box. "Can't we talk later—after the parade? I'm trying to concentrate."

Chester strutted forward, holding his head high. "Beagles," he said. "We were bred for marches. In England, the queen—"

"Not now, Chester. We need to worry about *our* queen!" Kito shook his head. His team was supposed to be sniffing out crime—not carrying on like this. "Dog Watch," he reminded Chester. "Tire slashed. Get your mind on—"

Muffin squeezed between them. "Chester, you're always makin' like you're some Englishman's hound. You were born here, not England. Your nose stays hitched up, clear to the clouds."

"I have my dignity," Chester said, trotting along and snatching a biscuit that nearly hit him in the nose. "My registration papers say it all."

"Means zip to me, sugar," Muffin answered, nipping at his ear. In turn, Chester tackled her out of the next biscuit.

Lucky hobbled closer. "I think I know who did the tire slashing," she whispered to Kito.

"You do?"

"Maybe the mayor's mother."

"Hmmm," Kito replied cautiously. He knew Lucky to be quick to judge without all the details. "That's a dog of a different color. Mothers don't usually—"

"What if she wanted the house to herself? It's one thing for a dog to live at home all his days, but with people, well, a man who lives with his mother and never moves on. . . . I think she sabotaged the parade so he wouldn't ride in Baby this year. Maybe get the message and move out. What do you think?"

"Uh, well," Kito said. "Maybe." But the idea didn't ring true to him. The mayor, who had a doctorate in psychology, probably never got around to leaving home, same way he never got around to learning how to drive. And what mother would turn out her own son, especially one who tossed out dog biscuits?

Crowds lined the streets as the parade passed the community building. Everyone waved and smiled at the dogs.

"There's my Lucky!" Lucky's owner yelled.

"Hi, Schmitty!" Schmitty turned his head and smiled.

"See?" Mr. H was pointing out his dogs to other people in the crowd. "There's our boys—Chester and Kito!"

They wagged their tails. The parade neared the post office, and with all the excitement, Kito forgot his worries for a moment and caught a green bone-shaped biscuit flying toward him. *Snap!* It was delicious. Maybe Schmitty was right. Better to think about problems after the parade.

Nothing like a good biscuit to—

Ssssssss—came the sudden sound of spraying water.

Ka-woooosh!!!—the fire hydrant sprayed, then exploded into a tidal wave of foamy white water that hit Mayor Jorgenson square in the face and knocked him clear off his feet, sending him flying. He lay dazed in a growing pool of swirling water. A foamy stream roared and shot from the hydrant. The whole parade came to a soggy, sloshing, disastrous halt.

14

Caught!

"**Dog Watch!**" Kito barked. "Sniff for clues. There must be fresh ones around here. This must have just happened."

Immediately Schmitty, Chester, Lucky, and Muffin rallied to his side. The other Pembrook dogs were busy scrambling after soggy biscuits in the water as Mayor Jorgenson sat up, dismay splattered across his face. Dogs barked, people scattered, and the hydrant continued to burst water.

Hopping over the water, the dogs raced around the hydrant, looking for any evidence of tampering. They scouted the stairs leading up to the post office, in case someone was hiding in the entry corner. They wove in and around wet parade goers. One child cried because her cotton candy had melted. "It's no-mo!" she yelled.

Within minutes water was threatening to flood the street.

"Don't let your instruments get ruined! Stay out of the water!" the band conductor shouted.

"I lost my baton! It floated away!"

The fire engine turned on its flashing lights and sirens and edged forward. Fire-fighters, faces wide with grins, jumped from the truck and ran to the hydrant. They quickly managed to shut off the water.

A calm fell over the scene.

"That was fun!" a child cried, and then stomped through the water.

Some of the dogs joined in. Kids and teenagers splashed and laughed. The parade may have been interrupted, but the cele-bration couldn't be stopped.

But Kito's back hairs stood on edge. Chester sniffed the air. Without a word, they headed toward the tavern and rounded the building, then found Gunnar pinning Mr. Cutler against the wall. Like an anchor, he was using his short but heavy basset-hound build and leaning against the village handyman's legs.

"Gunnar, stop!" Kito tried to warn Gunnar not to make the same mistake he'd made with Mr. Cutler. It wasn't worth getting grounded over mistaken identity. Mr. Cutler's new overalls probably confused Gunnar, too.

But then Kito saw things as they were. Mr. Cutler was holding the large wrench he'd used to stop the previous fire hydrant leak. If his tool could stop a leak, it could start one too.

Mr. Cutler's lower lip began to tremble. With his back against the wall, he slid down to a squatting position beside Gunnar. He put his free arm around Gunnar's neck.

"You dogs are my only true friends," he said, blubbering.

Gunnar gave Kito a questioning look. "He's acting like I'm his friend," he said, "but

he ran back here to hide, so I'm pinning him until someone decides what to do with him."

"Good dogs," wailed Mr. Cutler. "You're all good dogs—"

But the dogs met eyes and knew what they had to do. They each grabbed a corner of Mr. Cutler's new trousers, sunk their teeth into the dense fabric, and began pulling Mr. Cutler on his bottom all the way around the corner.

"What are you dogs doing?!" he cried out. "Stop that!"

But Dog Watch was in action. They pulled Mr. Cutler, who clenched the wrench firmly, all the way over to the fire hydrant, where the firefighters were clustered together.

"It was loosened on purpose," one said.

"Someone must have—," said another, and stopped.

The dogs delivered Mr. Cutler to the fire-fighters. He looked from the crowd to the wrench gripped in his hands. "Oh dear."

The mayor approached. Water squooshed from his tennis shoes as he walked. He

stopped by the dogs, who were not letting go of Mr. Cutler's trousers, despite his trying to wiggle away. The crowd pressed in around them.

"Mr. Cutler," the mayor asked. "I'm not sure what to make of this, but . . . is the water leak *your* doing?"

Mr. Cutler bowed his head. For a few seconds he was completely still, then he looked up, speaking to everyone around him. "Yes," he said stubbornly.

"Are you responsible for the power outages and banner vandalism too?"

Mr. Cutler shrugged, then nodded.

Everyone was silent.

Kito was stunned. How could Mr. Cutler find it in himself to do such things? And why?

Before Kito could ponder it any further, Mr. Cutler explained himself.

"I should have been the one to lead the parade today! We tied in the race for mayor—I lost the recount by a measly two votes. Probably yours and your mother's votes. I should have been mayor. It's not fair. . . . I couldn't stand watching the celebration, everyone having fun—"

Mayor Jorgenson rubbed his hand over his bald head, as if thinking of what to do next. "Hey," he said, "it's a hot day—a scorcher." He turned to the crowd. "A little shower felt great, right?"

The crowd murmured.

The mayor extended his hand to Mr. Cutler, who ignored it. "Dogs," the mayor said, "you can let go now."

Mr. Cutler brushed dog spit and wet dirt off his new overalls, and stood up on his own.

The mayor said, "Let's get on with our celebration. Pembrook is everyone's village, and you—Mr. Cutler—are a terrific handyman. Can we count on you to keep power supplied throughout the rest of the day?"

Mr. Cutler looked embarrassed and stunned. Then sheepishly, as he looked around the crowd from face to face, others began to laugh. Soon he started to smile too.

"Then join our parade," said the mayor.

The crowd cheered. Soon the parade was reorganized, the dogs were back in line and ready to catch biscuits, even if they were merely soggy crumbs, and despite the water in the streets, everything was seemingly back to normal.

"Dog Watch! Dog Watch!" Chester bayed.

"Got that right, sweetie!" Muffin called back.

Schmitty smiled so wide, his pink gums were showing.

Kito should have been happy. They had caught the culprit. At the critical moment, the dogs had worked together and brought justice and order back to the village. But how could he feel good when Tundra was still missing? He had the sinking, terrible feeling that perhaps they would never see her again—and his tail, which normally curled proudly over his back, drooped low.

Train Stop

As the parade headed for the tracks, a train whistle sounded—*Toooot! Tooooot!*—and a train engine pulling a long load of cargo cars chugged to a slower and slower pace, blocking the street.

The mayor held up his arm. "Hold up!" he cried, "we'll have to wait for this train."

"Noooo!" a child cried.

"Not another delay!"

"Nevvvvver seeeeeeen a parade liiiiike this!" Gunner said. With a shake of his head he sent drool strands flying.

Over the rolling din of train cars and the

squeaks and jangling of metal against metal, Kito heard something that made his ears prick up.

A high-pitched and long howl came from one of the cars approaching the intersection. It was a dog's despairing cry for help!

"Wa-ooooooooooo! Wa-oooooooooo!"

Kito barked twice, loud and sharp, to get the attention of the other dogs. "Follow me!"

Instantly the parade dogs followed his lead as he dashed toward the side of the moving train.

"Hey, dogs!" yelled the mayor. "Get back in line!" He shook the soggy box of dog biscuits over his head. But this time, the dogs didn't turn. They were intent on Kito's lead and the cry coming from a green boxcar.

Kito raced ahead toward the engine as it crawled slowly toward the depot and came to a stop. The engineer stepped out of his cab and stood on the steps. Kito barked and barked, turned in excited circles, barked some more, and dashed toward the green boxcar and back again.

The engineer flipped off his cap, scratched his head of black hair, then shrugged. He turned to the audience of parade goers, who were fanning out and coming closer to investigate what the dogs were up to.

"Seems this dog is trying to tell me something," the engineer said to the crowd, and stepped down to Kito.

The dogs were clustered together in front of the green boxcar, yipping and barking and jumping up and down. Now that the train had come to a stop, and the crowd was intent on something happening, an eerie quiet fell over the scene.

The mournful cry rang out clearly. "Wa-ooooooooooo! Wa-oooooooooooo!"

And the dogs knew beyond a shadow of a cat that the cry belonged to none other than their beloved Tundra. They began howling in chorus beside the boxcar door.

"All right, all right," the engineer said, stepping closer. "Make room now. I'll open it."

With a creak the door slid sideways, and there in an empty boxcar, looking a few

pounds heavier, stood Tundra. Her usually white coat was dingy gray, and she blinked as the sun hit her eyes. In a graceful arc she leaped from the boxcar into the throng of dogs, who were all sniffs, wags, and licks.

Mr. Erickson rushed forward, wearing a tall Uncle Sam hat. "Tundra!" he cried, kneeling before her and throwing his arms around her neck. Tears started at the corners of his eyes. "I thought I'd never see my girl again! What in the world were you doing in a boxcar?"

Tundra put her paws to Mr. Erickson's shoulders and licked his cheek over and over. As the crowd pressed around him, Mr. Erickson explained how he'd been searching for his dog with no luck.

"Well, she's back now," said Mavis, the postmaster. "That's what counts."

As the engineer returned to his cab and the train began rolling to Canada, Tundra joined the dogs beside Mayor Jorgenson, who was still holding up the wet box of biscuits. "Let's get back in formation," he said. "The parade isn't over yet."

Tundra sat down in front, and at her lead, all the other dogs followed, talking at once as they waited.

"What happened?"

"Where were yoooooou?"

"Someone steal ya, honey?"

"Was it Mr. Cutler?" Chester asked.

The train cleared the tracks and the parade continued.

Tundra caught a biscuit midair, then explained. "I followed a delicious scent the other day," she said, "right up from Seven Oaks Park to the train. When I found that the boxcar door was ajar, I jumped in. And you know what I found?"

"Someone luring you away?" Kito asked.

She smiled and gave her head a shake. "No, far less serious than that. Far better! A whole boxcar of dogfood. And not just any kind either. It was top-shelf stuff— bags and bags and bags of Supreme Doggie Delight!"

Schmitty snorted. "And to think I howled all night, sure that you were dead. Sorta embarrassing now."

Tundra butted his shoulder with her head. "Hey, at least you cared. No, seriously, one of the bags was torn and I started nibbling. Oh, it was good—a mixture of veal, lamb, and chicken. Perfect seasonings. Next thing I knew, well, the train jolted forward and the door slid shut."

"Someone locked you in?" Chester asked.

"No, I would have heard someone approach. The door just rolled on its own and locked with a clunk. The movement of the train, I suppose."

"Well then"—Chester shot Kito and Schmitty a sheepish look—"looks like we were barking up the wrong tree, so to speak. Thought someone was up to trouble puttin' you on that train."

"Oh, no," Tundra said. "Nothing that dramatic. A simple accident—though I must say, a rarity for me."

"So there you were, in total darkness,"

Muffin said sympathetically. "Oh, Tundra, sugar, were you scared?"

"Of course not. I had enough food to survive. I could think of worse situations for a dog to find herself in. When the car was unloaded, I hopped out, then followed the tracks toward home. I made it as far as Orr, when I stumbled upon an empty boxcar and a train stopping for repairs. It was turned north, so I figured—why not? When it slowed down, I listened—heard some of your voices and knew I was back in Pembrook, so I started howling—"

"Hoping someone would hear you?" Chester asked.

"Or howlin' 'cause you missed us?" Muffin stepped closer to Tundra, but not too close.

Tundra's normally white ears were dirt streaked and fly bitten. Her coat was filthy from riding the rails, yet she held her head high. She turned her focus to Mayor Jorgensons's biscuits. "Missed you all? Maybe a little."

Kito could barely believe his ears. Not in

all his days had he ever heard Tundra let on that she cared a lick for the other dogs. He shot Chester a glance and smiled. Their alpha dog was back at last.

Dog Watch Forever

The parade wound toward the village beach and back again past Erickson's Very Fine Grocery Store and Woody's Fairly Reliable Guide Service. It passed the bookstore and the coffee shop, Grandma's Restaurant and the railroad tracks, and ended near the post office. In the field between the post office and Seven Oaks Park, a colorful group of Ojibwe dancers gathered.

With silver jangles and in costumes from red to yellow to lavender, the powwow began. In a whirl of moccasins and tennis shoes, the dancers circled the drummers, who added their voices to the pounding of the large drums.

"Oh, count me in!" cried Chester.

"Music to my bassyyyyet hoooooound ears," said Gunnar. And the two set off. In seconds they were seated—rumps down and snouts up—howling in chorus.

Schmitty, Kito, and Tundra joined the crowd and looked on.

"Y'know," Kito said, "the Native Americans were here long before this became Pembrook."

"You got that right," Schmitty added.

"Yes, and dogs," Tundra said, her head high, "were right here with the earliest people."

"I'm sure you're right," Schmitty said, "but how do you know that?"

"History Channel. I watched a program on dogs once. We go way, way, way back."

Kito knew it was true. He'd read something like that in a dog book, but he kept his sources to himself.

Later that afternoon, bellies full from left-over corn dogs, giant pretzels, and popcorn, Chester and Kito were strolling around booths and grabbing an occasional lap of water at the beach.

"Hey," Chester said. "Check out the fire hydrant."

Mr. Cutler was squatting beside it, with several cans of paint nearby and a paint-brush in hand. "Let's check it out," said Kito.

They gathered at his heels and sat down to watch.

The fire hydrant was no longer bright yellow. Now it resembled a doll with a face wearing a red and blue outfit. "I don't get it," Chester said.

"It's Raggedy Ann," explained Kito. "I've read—I mean, I saw her in a book once that a child was reading aloud."

"I still don't get it," Chester said, tilting his head sideways and pricking up his ears where they folded near his head.

"You dogs probably wonder what I'm up to," Mr. Cutler said, glancing at them.

"Got that right," said Chester, but of course, Mr. Cutler couldn't hear him and continued on.

"People might think it's a little strange, but I guess this is my way of saying I'm sorry and starting all over again." He added black eyelashes to Raggedy Ann's face, then switched paintbrushes and dabbed red on her cheeks. Kito would never have guessed that Mr. Cutler was an artist, too.

Then Mr. Cutler sat back on his heels, arms over his chest, admiring his handiwork. "There, that's better" he said, and stood. He brushed off his overalls and tapped the lids back on his paint cans. "Hope people like it."Then he headed back to the garage at the community building.

Chester kept staring. "I like it. She's awfully cute."

"Chester,"Kito said."She's a fire hydrant."

Schmitty and Tundra trotted up to them, and Chester explained the new design on their fire hydrant.

"I see,"Tundra said,"but why—I still don't get why Mr. Cutler was apologizing."

The dogs explained how their search for Tundra had helped them to stumble on someone's plans to ruin the village celebration and how, just before Tundra's return, they had caught Mr. Cutler red-handed.

"Well then," Tundra said, "that certainly explains the new paint job."

"When things started to look suspicious," Kito continued, "we put our noses together about how we could keep a better watch on our village. . . ."

All sniffs and wags, Kito, Chester, and Schmitty filled Tundra in on their new idea for protecting the dogs and people of Pembrook.

"Dog Watch," she repeated, as if weighing the value of the idea.

Kito waited anxiously, tail dipped slightly downward. If Tundra didn't like their plan, then there would be nothing they could do to revive it again. Among the dogs, she always had the last word—and it was law.

"Hmmm . . . Dog Watch . . . ," she said again, but this time with a quick wag of her tail. A wag so quick he'd nearly missed it, but Kito knew in that moment that she really liked the idea.

"Well then, we better get to work," she said. "The celebration isn't over yet, and who knows when we might be needed next. Bring me up to speed on all the details about this new plan, and don't leave out a single thing. . . ."

Schmitty, Chester, and Kito wagged their tails with enthusiasm. Then talking all at once, they trotted off together with Tundra toward Seven Oaks Park, where the evening festivities were taking place.

In the dusk people young and old gathered on blankets and in lawn chairs near the shore. Some dogs sat with their owners, while others played tug-of-war with sticks or wrestled in the grass beneath the oak trees. But when the first fireworks whistled overhead, everyone—dogs and people—stopped what they were doing and watched as the sky erupted into a shower of green and purple and yellow sparks.

Chester and Kito settled on a fuzzy plaid blanket between the Hollinghorsts. As the next fireworks screeched into the sky, Kito jumped, ready to run home, but he felt Mr. H's warm and assuring hand on his back. "It's okay, fella," he said. "You don't need to worry. It's just fireworks."

Kito let out a deep sigh. He rested his head

on his paws. At the shoreline, firefighters took turns setting off the display. Shimmering lights lit up the night sky and cascaded down in a rainbow of colors. For the moment—all was well in Pembrook.